Identified

Emily Hemstock

DEDICATION

In dedication to Jesus...

CONTENTS

ACKNOWLEDGMENTS

Daddy,
You've always encouraged me to write.
Our daddy-daughter breakfast dates
were inspiration for this story.

Joe & Heidi Hemstock, Marla Tuinstra,
Angela Musser and Brenda Musser,
my amazing proof reading team:
thank you so much for your dedication
and time invested in this project.
I can't thank you enough!

Mary Jansen,
You were the first fiction-writer author I ever met.
You inspired me in ways I can't even count.
Thank you for helping me believe that dreams do come true.

DEDICATION:

*for my fam: Daddy, Mom, Hannah & Jordan,
Aaron, Rachel, Nathan, Josiah, Zac, and Bethany.*

1 THE ENCOUNTER

(Chloe)

Menominee High School…the place where, sometime between now and when my tassel is flipped, I am supposed to grow up; and, at some indefinite moment – I'm magically supposed to know who I am, and what I want to do for the rest of my life.

I sure wish I knew now. Especially now.

"Chloe, what do you want to be when you grow up?" First of all, who asks a sophomore anything 'when they grow up'?

We're clearly already grown up. Mostly.

Apparently, Mr. Grill, teacher of my College Preparation class, asks questions like that.

"Uhm." I started, but had no answer.

"Do you have a college in mind?"

"I'm still thinking about it."

"Well, students," he began, "this is a perfect example of each of you. High school is not a big social party. In two short years, you will be in the real world. Before our next class, I'd like each of you to think of two career possibilities. Class dismissed."

I could feel my face getting hot. He really didn't have

to embarrass me in front of the whole class, did he?

In the hallway, Faith Peters walked up to me. She took my arm in her hand.

"Chloe, don't feel bad. None of us know what we're doing when we graduate."

Faith is the absolute best friend I could ever ask for. We've been friends since kindergarten. Sometimes, I feel like she knows me better than I even know myself.

"Thanks, bestie."

Faith let go of my arm and adjusted her backpack. She was quick to change the subject: "Did you hear about Avery Salazar?"

"Nope."

"He got in trouble for drugs in his locker."

"Dude." I said, impressed. How does Faith get the latest gossip anyway?

"I know, right? He's in so much trouble."

"Did they check all the lockers?" I asked. "I feel like there are a lot of people who would get in trouble."

"Two others got suspended. I don't know their names."

"There's more." Faith's eyes were glowing with anticipation. I love her to death, but she loves to gossip. I struggled through my backpack to find my essay, only half interested in what she had to say.

"It's about you," she teased.

The bell rang signifying the starting of next period. I should be seated in the front-row desk of Mrs. Anderson's English class, if I ever plan to get my tassel flipped.

"Tell me, quick." I started walking toward classroom 111. I didn't realize how quiet the halls had become while Faith and I were talking. There was a slight echo as Faith began to talk.

"The latest is that you are joining The Lions."

I laughed. Literally LOL-ed. 'The Lions' is a stupid juvenile gang, if you can even call it a gang. It's basically a group of kids in and out of juvenile detention who listen to Avery Salazar as if he's a king.

"That's a good one, Faith."

"No," said Faith, "I'm one-hundred percent serious."

I stared into her green eyes. She wasn't kidding.

***

The front door of our Victorian-styled home slammed shut behind me.

"Chloe, is that you? I'm in the kitchen."

"Yes." I placed my backpack down at the stair entry and walked through the living room to the kitchen.

Mom was standing next to the island rolling pie crust out on the counters smooth surface. She had an apron over her adorable white blouse and blue, fifties-style skirt. A small section of hair that wiggled its way out of her gorgeous French twist, hung elegantly over the left side of her face. My mom was stunning.

"Chloe. You need to take the driveway slower."

"Oh." I suddenly found the ceiling very interesting. I never noticed that spaghetti noodle. Oh wait. I threw it there yesterday to see if my pasta dinner was done.

She narrowed her gaze at me, "I'm being serious."

I looked into her eyes and smiled. "Ok, mom. I will."

I was eager to change the subject. I didn't want mom and dad to get any ideas about taking me off their insurance.

"What's for dinner?" I asked her.

"We're having fried chicken for dinner with apple pie for dessert."

"Sounds delicious, as usual," I said.

I took my apron off the hook and began to help. Mom chattered about her office job as we finished the last few preparations of dinner and then she sent me to get dad.

The door was slightly open when I got to his office. Dad was on the phone. I didn't mean to eaves drop, but when I heard my name I subconsciously crept closer.

"Yes sir, Chloe would be more than capable of it. I'm only worried about her safety." Dad paused as the other person talked. I couldn't make out what he was saying but it sounded like a male voice.

"I know you have other agents in her school," he paused again, "I'd like to think about it. I'll let you know," he paused again. "Yes. You too. Bye."

What would I be capable of? Other agents in my school?

I was almost afraid to open the door all the way. I waited a second and then gently knocked on the door.

"Come in," Dad called. I poked my head in the door.

My dad sat behind his big oak desk.

His kind brown eyes were twinkling as he spoke, "It's my favorite daughter!"

"I'm your only daughter." I laughed.

"So, come tell me about your day."

I sat perched on the edge of his desk telling him all about class with Mr. Grill. Dad is literally one of my best friends; he always has good advice. I was sure he was going to be like, "of course, Mr. Grill was out of line" however; he just smiled.

"Maybe your Mr. Grill has a point after all. You're graduating in two years."

What? But I have no idea...

"Chloe!" Mom called from the kitchen, "I said to get your dad – not chatter his ear off while dinner is getting cold."

Dad and I laughed. Poor mom, I'd forgot all about dinner.

During dinner, however, I couldn't fully enjoy the deliciousness. Mr. Grill's voice plagued me.

Chloe, what do you want to be when you grow up?

***

Friday morning, I sat in my twenty-year old mustang behind the school in the parking lot. It's a pretty decent car, besides the Upper Peninsula rust factor. The muffler probably needs to be replaced because it sounds like a bomb, my headlights need adjusting, and there are coffee stains on the carpet... but, at least my heat still works. I warmed by hands by the vent, dreading the dash between my beater car and the cool brick building.

I scanned Menominee High, remembering how I was sure it was the most terrifying place in the whole wide world on my first day as a freshman. However, I've become accustom to the crowded hallways, unique style, and cold classrooms. It's hard to believe in two more years I'll be gazing at a new brick building – if I can ever decide in which college I should enroll.

I slid out of my mustang, my back pack slung over one shoulder. One of these days, I'm going to need a shoulder replacement. Teachers should really consider these things before they give me all this homework.

Faith opened one of the 10 maroon doors at the entrance.

"Hey, Chloe." As she spoke, she adjusted the backpack hanging on her left shoulder; apparently, I wasn't the only one having problems with the weight of school.

"Hey."

When my eyes adjusted to the hallway lighting, I saw the usual: tired teens scrambling to their classes, and teachers seeking refuge in their lounge.

Faith said something, but because we were passing the gym where the band class was practicing for the concert tonight, I didn't catch it.

"What? Sorry, I couldn't hear you."

"I was just saying, The Lions are…"

A voice called from behind me. "Chloe!"

I turned around to see my least favorite person: Sophia. Don't get me wrong, I don't exactly hate her; however, we definitely aren't friends. She's cheer captain, but she thinks her title is school captain.

"Chloe. I want you on the squad. Why didn't you try out?"

I considered telling her the truth: because I don't like her or her clicks. They're rude and stuck up. But, I didn't figure it would be very Christianly of me.

"I don't want to be a cheerleader, Sophia. But thank you for asking." I flashed, what I hoped was, a convincing smile.

Sophia came closer and lowered her voice. "Chloe, this kills my pride. I'm almost begging you. My only other option is Ana. Have you seen her lately?"

"Sophia, be nice." I said. It didn't matter to anyone that Ana was on medication which made her gain weight. But this is high school for you: cruel.

"She's like four-hundred pounds and dyed her hair pink. That's not going on my squad," Sophia snootily stuck her nose in the air.

"Well," I said decidedly, "I'm not either."

"You have the perfect sassy attitude and school pride. You're not three-hundred pounds overweight and you don't have pink hair. We would have to put you on the bottom of the pyramid because you are a little bigger than the girls and me. I wouldn't sweat it though, a little curve is good."

"How many times do I have to say 'no'?" I asked, walking away. *Did she just call me fat? I have a sassy attitude?*

"Please!" Sophia was all-but-on-her-knees begging. She stopped suddenly. "Wow, girl. When did you lose your glasses? Your eyes are gorgeous."

Really? They were? Oh wait. She's just using flattery again.

"And, oh my gosh. Who is your hair stylist? I never realized how long and smooth your hair was."

"Flattery isn't going to change my mind, Sophia. I'm not joining the team."

Sophia's attitude changed all grumpy.

"Why are you asking me now? Tryouts were a long time ago," I said.

"Because, one of the best girls on the team is moving to Marinette and I need to replace her," Sophia sighed. Marinette was our neighboring city. We have one football game together each year: The M&M game. It's been a city rivalry for over 100 years. I know it would kill Sophia if their squad had a better cheer than hers.

"Well, good luck," I said.

Because of my little run-in with Sophia, I was late to College Preparation. Of course, as soon as I opened the door, Mr. Grill stopped speaking and stared at us. Consequently, the whole class turned around; like one giant spinning ride at the carnival.

"Come in, girls. Next time, try not to be late." Mr. Grill motioned to a desk.

Faith and I took seats in the back row near our best friends, Christian Johnson, Jordan Herald and Ryan Jones. I've known them even longer than I've known Faith. Our families have attended the same church since before any of us were born.

Christian passed me a note. I quickly read it and passed it to Faith.

Dinner at Ryan's house. 5 p.m.

I slightly turned in my seat and made eye contact with

Ryan. I mouthed the word, "Yes".

"… we'll share what career options we've been exploring." Mr. Grill was talking. I was scared he was asking me. I totally zoned out with the whole note thing.

I looked around the room. Nobody was talking.

It was silent.

I hate silence.

"Mr. Grill. Can I go first?" I asked.

"Yes. But perhaps we should do it at the end of class, like I said a few seconds ago."

Someone in the back laughed.

I turned around and glared at… Avery? Wasn't he in detention or something?

I flipped Christian's note over and scribbled, *what is he doing here?* I shoved it to Faith's desk.

***

Monday morning started out as a beautiful day. The February's snow was melting, and the icicles were dripping from the roof of our Victorian home. The wind was oddly warm, especially for our section of the Upper Peninsula.

I lounged downstairs for some breakfast. Mom was just pulling fresh banana muffins out of the oven. It smelled like heaven.

"Thanks, Mom!" I said reaching for a muffin.

"No, you don't," Mom laughed, "they have to cool. Go to dad's office for a minute. I think he wants to talk with you."

My father sat at his desk gazing out the open window which overlooked the dancing leaves. The wind blew through the window and rumpled the envelope marked 'classified' that sat on his desk.

He spilled out the content of the envelope and stared hard at the information. His face held the gravity of a man trying to decide.

My grey sandals padded the carpeted floor as I made my way to his desk.

"How's my beautiful daughter this morning?"

"Wonderful." I adjusted my knee-length floral skirt and sat on the edge of his desk.

"What's up?" I asked as I looked around his office. Every detail was organized. He's a lawyer and usually he can work from home. He has an office on first street. His administrative assistant, Matthew Dillion, is usually the only one in his office. Dad says he works best at home, but needs the office downtown for publicity reasons.

"Mom said you wanted to see me?"

"Yes, could you drop off a file for Matthew? It's too confidential to e-mail."

I was secretly happy. Dad trusted me more than an e-mail.

"Sure thing." I grinned.

"Oh, and Chloe. I'm taking you out for dinner, so don't plan anything with your friends. I have something I need to talk to you about."

2 THE MISSION

Faith planned a night at the bowling alley during College Preparation. I hope there are no finals in this class, because I don't think anyone will pass. Mr. Grill just goes on and on these tangents, and they're hard to follow. Eventually, most of the students get so distracted, they resort to passing notes and sneaking peaks at their iPhones.

"Since we didn't get to all the students last class period, I'd like to begin where we left off with sharing our career options," Mr. Grill spoke.

He looked at me, and suddenly I realized I didn't have two career options.

"Let's start with…" I tried in vain to kick Ryan who sat behind me. Out of all my friends, Ryan is the only one who knows what he's doing when he graduates. He wants to be a pastor, like his dad. Unfortunately, my short five feet-six-inch self couldn't reach his desk. "… Chloe. Since she was so eager to begin last time."

Why had I been eager? Oh yeah, because I hate awkward silences. I really need to break this habit.

The whole class, as if in one motion, turned to me. My palms got sweaty, and suddenly it was hard to swallow.

"I've thought about being a teacher," I noticed a smile on Mr. Grill's face as I spoke. Maybe he didn't hate me after all. "However, I think I want to do something concerning the law practice. Kind of like my dad, Nathan Wyatt."

Mr. Grill smiled. "Good."

A rubber band whizzed past my head and bounced off the corner of Mr. Grill's desk. Needless to say, Avery Salazar and his gang were visiting the principal's office. Again.

In English class, Mrs. Anderson sent me to the office to pick up the assignment she'd forgot there. I welcomed the distraction. We're studying English Composition and it feels like we're writing a million essays.

Just as I was approaching the office, I heard someone behind me call my name.

I turned around to see Avery Salazar.

"Did you just get out of the principal's office?" I asked, fully knowing I was walking on thin ice.

Avery looked like a tomato about to burst into tomato sauce.

"It's none of your business."

"Well, I don't have my lunch money if that's what you're after. It gets safely deposited from my bank to the school account."

Avery was a big guy. He was 6'5" and about 250 pounds. He gets away with a lot because he intimidates students and sometimes even teachers. He scares me; however, I don't show it because it would just make him feel more tough.

"I don't want your lunch money, Wyatt."

"Well, what do you want?"

"You're a hard person to find alone, Ms. Social Butterfly."

"Yeah, well I try not to be with the school bully alone. So, if you'll excuse me."

"I won't."

Why did he look so big and scary? Calm down, Chloe.

"I heard you wanted to join The Lions. We have tough standards, and we've never had a girl pass them."

"What about Ashley Ground?" I asked referring to Avery's ex-girlfriend. She used to hang out with The Lions constantly.

"She ain't in the gang anymore."

"Isn't," I corrected.

"I don't need a grammar lesson from you of all people," he scuffed.

I shrugged. "I'm not sure where you got your facts from, Avery, but I'm not interested in joining your stupid gang."

"You have until Monday to decide. Meet me by the football field at nine."

"I'll be in class." I said quickly.

"Duh, genius, I mean at night."

"Absolutely not, I'm not completely stupid," I said, but Avery had already walked away.

***

Dad met me at the door with a smile on his face.

"My sweet baby girl is home!" He wrapped me in a big bear hug.

"Hey daddy!"

"Are you ready for dinner?" He asked.

"Almost. I need to go change from my sweaty school clothes."

I ran up the wooden stairs which led to my bedroom. I scrambled through a pile of clean clothes, wishing I'd taken the time this weekend to organize them. I settled on a black maxi dress I bought at an online boutique. I slipped a red belt around my waist and finished my outfit off with red fur boots.

We went to the family restaurant down the road. The place is so cute. It's the perfect small-town diner. It has old fashion décor with pictures of how Menominee used to look.

We took a seat overlooking the bay.

"Chloe."

I looked up from my menu. Dad was such a sweet person. Even if he wasn't my dad, I think we'd be great friends. I am so blessed. Not every girl has a dad who spends time with her.

"You've really grown up," he said.

His words mixed with the lull of the customer's conversation and the clanking of dishes.

I laughed. "I guess, despite my best efforts."

"I am so proud of you. You've done excellent in school, and all around, you're just a wonderful girl."

"Thanks, Daddy." I smiled.

The waitress set the food in front of us and we said grace.

I began to babble about my dreams of working with law enforcement. While I told him about the latest action movie I watched, Dad just smiled and listened.

"If you could spy in real life, would you?" Dad asked.

"Of course." I said without skipping a beat.

"Just remember not to spy on me when I'm working on a case or planning your birthday party." He laughed and then got serious, "Would you like a real spy job?"

My jaw dropped.

Dad went on to explain the local sheriff department put him in charge of a new program called ANTI. It stands for Action Nation Teen Interference. It's a program to help stop vandalism, bullying and drug dealing in the local high schools and colleges. The spies nose around to get as much information as they can, and then they report to their captain, who in my case would be dad. The bad guys never know who the spies are, and the spies never take matters in their own hands.

"That is so exciting! Are there other spies in my

school?"

"Yes, but you're not allowed to know who they are. The spies are not allowed to talk to each other. You're my daughter, which means I'm going to be twice as hard on you, especially in safety. You report everything to me, and you never take action."

"Okay."

"Do you know who The Lions are?"

"Yes, who doesn't?"

"Then you probably know they're into vandalism and bullying." I nodded as dad continued, "You may not know they're getting a little more serious. They're your target. You, and the other agents, are going to find out what they're up to; the only thing we've heard is a date, February 29."

"There are already rumors about me joining them."

"They were supposed to wait until I agreed to it." Dad said, irritation showed in his voice.

"You mean the agency is spreading the rumors?" I asked shocked.

"Yes," explained dad, "the other spies in your school were told to spread rumors and then the gang would probably approach you."

"So, I'm actually supposed to meet Avery tonight?" I asked.

***

That evening, dad and I drove to Menominee High School parking lot.

"Chloe, if you suspect trouble tell me right away. I'm there in seconds," Dad said; a serious expression clouded over his face. He looked like he was dropping me off for my first day of kindergarten.

"Okay, Daddy, remember, I know self-defense."

I shut the door and walked to the field. It was dark

already and stars hung down in the moonless sky. A silent, cool wind blew against my coat; I hugged my arms and tried not to shiver.

I stopped in the shadows of the brick school. Not a human was in sight.

"Great," I said, "I'm out here freezing for nothing."

A moment later I heard the snow crunch behind me. I slowly turned to see Avery Salazar standing in the shadows. It was slightly unnerving to see the school bully, alone, at night.

"I said the football field."

"Well. I'm in the parking lot." I stated the obvious.

We awkwardly stood there for a second. I slowly began to realize I felt no fear around Avery. He's just a kid. This wasn't the aggressive beast the whole school knew. He seemed different tonight, it was like I got to see a different side of him.

"So, do you want to join the gang?" Avery shifted his feet in the snow. Every ounce of good girl in my heart begged me to say no.

"I might be interested," I spoke calmly.

"Listen kid, either you are, or you're not," Avery snapped.

"What's the initiation? I'll show you I'm serious."

"I want you to break into the principal's office tomorrow, and get the grade sheet. I'm assuming you know how to pick a lock?"

"Well, now that you've mentioned it," I paused, "not really."

"Figures," he said under his breath, "you are a good girl, aren't you?"

"My criminal résumé could use a little help. I've been a good girl," I paused, "so far."

"Are you sure you want to get your hands dirty? You

might break a nail."

"Please. I'm sick of always trying to please people. If I'm already disappointing people, I might as well have fun with it." I think I saw that line on a movie, because I am way too 'good girl' to ever come up with it.

Avery looked like he actually understood me.

"You can swipe a set of keys from the janitor." Avery said.

"Okay thanks." I said.

"Thanks?" Avery questioned, then he turned and walked away, "Whatever, kid."

***

My heart was thumping loudly. This was, not only the first time I stole keys, but also the first time I was in the principal's office. It was freaky, especially since I was alone in the office and wasn't supposed to be there. I've had few run-ins with Mr. Stevens, our principal, and I'd like to keep it that way; he kind of scares me. I was literally praying he wouldn't walk through the door.

I took a grade sheet from the top of his desk. I was out of there. I was so ready to leave. I opened the door, hoping nobody was watching.

"Chloe?"

I spun around. Ryan stood in the hall with a perplexed look on his face.

I started to walk away.

"I saw you, Chloe." He took a step closer.

"Ryan," I whispered, "This is not what it looks like."

"Chloe." He must have spotted the grade sheet in my hand. I shoved it behind my back and walked away but he stepped in front of me.

"Ryan." I avoided eye contact.

"What is going on? Are you okay?"

"Please, Ryan," I begged, "I'm okay."

"Yeah, you sure look it."

I sighed, trying to decide what to do. I knew what he must be thinking. "You don't understand. Please don't tell on me."

He opened his mouth, but no words came out.

I looked up and felt the blood draining from my face. Avery Salazar stood behind Ryan, his iPhone out capturing the whole scene.

"Avery Salazar," I gasped.

3 THE BODY GUARD

I dropped the grade sheet and stared at the two boys. Avery stood with his feet a shoulders length apart, arms crossed and a determined look on his face.

Ryan looked much smaller in comparison.

"Chloe, why do you hang out with this twerp? You're much too pretty for him."

I jumped at how aggressive Avery's voice sounded.

"Leave Chloe out of this, Salazar." Ryan said.

"She brought herself into this, didn't you Chloe?"

"Yeah, but it's not what it seems..." I started but Avery cut me off.

"Face it, preacher boy, she's not your type." I cringed. Ryan's father pastors the biggest church in our community. In school, the troublemakers refer to him as 'preacher boy'. I think it bothers Ryan that they assume he's a saint.

"I can replay the video of her breaking into the office if you need convincing," Avery said.

"You're a freak!" I fumed. I pushed past Ryan and walked up to Avery. I stood inches from his face.

"Watch what you call me, princess," Avery said, "or this may just end up in the wrong hands."

"Leave her alone," Ryan said, he took my hand and gently eased me away from Avery.

The tension in the hall was so thick, I was finding it hard to breathe.

For a long moment, nobody said anything.

Avery's voice shattered the silence like a rock hitting

glass, "I'll see you later, Chloe."

Avery walked down the hall. His footsteps echoed fear into me. I stared at the floor. I definitely owed Ryan an explanation.

"Let's go outside and get some air," Ryan said, "if you're feeling up to it."

"Yeah," I whispered, "but first I need to return these."

I said, staring grimly at the keys on the ground.

Ryan picked them up with his left hand, that's when I realized he was still holding mine with the other. He must have too, because he slowly let go of my hand and slipped the keys in his pocket.

We brought the keys to the janitor's closet and put them on the floor underneath the key rack; an obvious place where the janitor would find them.

We started walking towards our neighborhood. I knew I had to tell Ryan something, but I didn't know how much I could. Ryan's cell phone rang, slicing through the icy silence. He answered it and I could tell from the conversation that it was his mom.

"Chloe," he said after he hung up, "Alexa and mom just got a flat tire; can we meet later and talk?"

"I don't really want to."

"Chloe," Ryan stopped walking, "if it's not what it seems, why can't you tell me?"

"I can't tell you why."

Ryan stopped walking. "You're like my best friend. If you're in trouble, I want to help. Why can't you trust me?"

"Fine. I'll call you tonight. I'll talk."

"Do you mind if I still walk you home?" Ryan asked.

"What about your mom and sister?" I asked.

"Your house is on the way."

Dad wasn't in his office when I got home. Mom, who met me in the kitchen, said he was at a business dinner and wouldn't be home until late.

"Can I cook a pizza?" I asked. Mom eyed me skeptically.

"Last time you cooked, I came home to a smoky kitchen. I'll cook the pizza."

"Thank you, Mom, you're the best."

"Cheese?" She asked as she walked into the kitchen and opened the freezer door.

"Yes, thank you."

"I swear, Chloe, one day you're going to turn into a frozen pizza."

Immediately after dinner, I went up in my room. I tried to distract myself with social media and video games. It didn't work, so I eventually ended up calling Ryan. He said he'd stop by in twenty minutes.

I threw my iPhone on my bed and headed to my walk-in closet. I searched the back corner until I found my favorite dress boots. I slid my feet into them and walked to the hall mirror.

"Where are you going?" Mom asked when she met me in the hall.

"Ryan is picking me up and we're going to go talk." I said. I slipped into my leather jacket.

"I knew you guys would end up going out… sooner or later." Mom teased.

"Please, Mom. This is not a date."

The doorbell rang. I ran/tripped down the stairs in a super un-lady like fashion.

"Girl," Mom called, "settle down. It's not a date, remember?"

I opened the door. Ryan was wearing his cowboy boots, designer jeans and a plaid blue button-up shirt.

This wasn't a date, right?

"Do you want some hot chocolate? We can stop at

Coffee Corner." He walked around to my side of his truck and opened the door for me.

This wasn't a date, right? No. It was just two friends going out.

"That sounds great," I said. He knew Coffee Corner was my favorite place in town.

The café was on First Street in downtown Menominee; it overlooked the beautiful Green Bay of Michigan.

We pulled into the parking lot and walked on the white, wooden porch that hugged the little house.

The aroma of freshly baked sweets immediately filled my lungs as we walked through the open wooden door. We were soon seated in a booth in the back of the café.

The waitress brought the coffee we ordered. We silently sat staring at each other.

Finally, Ryan spoke up.

"Chloe, if you need to talk, I'm always here."

I quietly smiled, choking down some emotion with a sip of my latte.

"Well, I don't know how much I'm allowed to say," I said. Ryan nodded slowly, but didn't speak. "I really don't know what to say."

"Why did you break into the office today?" Ryan asked gently after a pause.

"Avery told me to do it," I said, very conscious of how lame it sounded.

"Why did Avery tell you to?" Ryan looked at me, his blue eyes shone innocence. I knew I couldn't lie to him.

"I can't talk about it. I promise I'll tell you as soon as I can," I said.

Ryan sighed and sat back in his chair. "Chloe, I'm your friend. I love you and want what's best for you. You can't get caught up in that gang, girl."

"I know how it looks, just please, trust me. I know what I'm doing."

'I think,' I mentally added.

"I want to trust you You've never given me a reason not to trust you," Ryan's response cut deep. I could just imagine what he was thinking of me right now. He spoke again. "I'm sorry for being so pushy. If I trust you, which I do, I need to allow you to tell me in your time."

"Thanks, Ryan."

We drank the rest of our drinks in a peaceful silence.

"Do you want to walk down to the beach?" I asked.

The bell on the door rang as we left the café.

"Ryan, thank you for caring enough to talk with me."

"I wasn't kidding in there," he paused on the porch, "I love you. More than you'll ever know. I want what's best for you."

I was suddenly uncomfortable with this conversation. *He loved me, more than I'll ever know? He was talking friends, right? Of course, he was. Wasn't he?*

"Right back at you, Ryan." It was quiet a moment. "I'll race you to the water."

We kicked up the sand mixed with snow behind us in a flurry whirl as we raced. We walked on the beach until darkness crept over the watery horizon. Then, we made our way to the metal swing set overlooking the water. We swayed for some time in the quietness of the evening. The occasional creaking of the chains made beat to the rhythm of an unknown song.

A motor revved in the parking lot behind us. I glanced over my shoulder and saw a black convertible hidden in the shadows.

"Ryan," I said, "It's getting late. I should get home."

I don't know why, but something about that convertible made me uncomfortable.

A lone owl hooted. In the shadows, someone coughed. I stood and tightened my grip on the swing chains, "I want to go home."

"Chloe," He whispered my name softly. "It'll be okay." Nevertheless, we walked back up to Ryan's truck.

By the time we got there I was feeling pretty stupid. I opened my mouth to apologize for being a cry baby when I felt someone roughly grab my coat sleeve. Unfortunately, for the person, I'm a black belt in karate. I spun around and instinctively planted a kick to his jaw. Avery Salazar fell to the ground with an earth shattering thud.

He cussed and stood up, looking as angry as a beast. Avery lowered his head and started at me. He looked like defense on our football team.

"You're gonna pay for this, kid."

I reeled back hitting Ryan's truck. All the calmness I'd felt that time I met him in the baseball field was shattering into pieces.

Ryan came from around the front of the truck. "What's going on?"

"Just who do you think you are, punk, her bodyguard or something?" Avery growled.

"Cool off, Salazar."

Avery answered by throwing a punch at Ryan, and Ryan blocked the punch and stepped back.

"You chicken, preacher boy?"

"No, Salazar. I just don't take to fighting in front of ladies."

"Then maybe the lady wants to fight."

"Keep your hands off her, Salazar." Ryan chuckled, "Plus it looks like she already threw you down."

Avery took a step closer to me. I took a deep breath, trying to remember the moves that made throwing a guy three times your size easy.

Ryan stepped between us. "Pick on someone your own size, Salazar."

I'd never seen Ryan fight. Except in football. Avery took another step toward me. Ryan answered by using one of his tackle moves on Avery and told me to get in the truck. Ryan had Avery pinned, when out of the corner of my eye, I saw a man in a black jacket approach from the shadows. Before I could yell a warning, he had a pistol between Ryan's shoulder blades.

"Put your hands up, preacher boy."

"Who are you?" I asked.

"Shut up, lady. Or your boyfriend won't live to tell about it."

Ryan slowly stood with his hands lifted. I was praying someone would see the scene and call the police officers.

This suddenly turned from a high school fight to a life or death situation. My eyes watered. What if this mystery man killed Ryan? Ryan was just trying to help me. He took me out tonight to see if I was okay. I was so selfish. He told me he loved me and cared about me. I never told him… What if he died tonight? Without knowing I loved him? I'd been in this all-out denial for relationships in general. I'd been totally cool with the friend-zone forever. But suddenly, I wanted Ryan to know I cared about him. I wanted him to know he was my best friend too.

"Ryan…"

Avery slowly rose from the sidewalk. He walked to me.

"Chloe, you're a faker. This is serious stuff. I can't let twerps like you ruin it for us." He put his hands on my shoulders and looked me in the eye.

"Don't you dare hurt her, Salazar. I swear I'll kill you if you do." Ryan said through clenched teeth.

The mystery man spoke low, "You are in no place to be making threats."

My attention was on Avery, and how close he was standing to me.

"Who told you?" I whispered.

"So, it is true, double-crossing-" Avery started but I interrupted him.

"I didn't say that."

"Do you know what I do to double crossers like you?"

"Do you know what the police do to guys like you?" I asked. I knew my voice was trembling with fear, but I would not cower to this jerk.

"This is exactly why you'll never get to them."

Avery was now towering over me. I glanced around him; Ryan was still struggling.

"Face it, kid. You lose."

Everything went dark.

***

I groaned and reached to ease the pain in my head.

"Hold still," a low voice said.

I squirmed again until something slammed me back on my pillow. I tried to struggle through the groggy dream and wake up, but it didn't work.

Someone slammed a car door. A motor started.

There were more voices.

"Salazar, take care of these kids. Do you know what I mean? I don't want them meddling again."

"What do you want me to do with them?" The fearful male voice sounded so familiar. Who was he? What was going on?

"Here's my gun. Make it look like an accident or something. Better yet, frame one of them."

"Gillis. I am not a murderer."

"You are whatever I say you are. If you know what's good for you."

Suddenly, the vehicle in which I was sitting lurched forward. Tires squealed. It took me a moment to realize I was in the moving vehicle, and not in my bed dreaming.

How did I get here?

It was like the deafening fear of a nightmare, and the sinking realization I couldn't wake up from this dream.

Through my blurry vision, I recognized Ryan's truck. I was lying on the back seat.

I quietly sighed in relief. If Ryan was here, I'll be okay.

Suddenly, I realized the guy driving wasn't Ryan.

I slowly sat up, trying to be quiet. Ryan wasn't in the front seat. In fact, he was nowhere to be seen.

I dropped my feet to the floor, only to realize something was down there.

Someone.

I bend down and touched Ryan's arm.

I didn't dare say anything. I was afraid the driver would

hear me.

I traced my hand down the side of his face until I could feel his breath.

Good. At least he's alive.

The driver still hadn't noticed I was up.

I had to think fast. What was I going to do? We were now approaching what I recognized to be Highway M-35. The driver accelerated. We were going farther and farther away from civilization; I had to do something fast.

I considered grabbing the wheel and turning Ryan's truck into the ditch. Sure, he'd probably hate me for wrecking his brand-new truck he worked all summer to pay for… but at least we'd be alive.

Or would we? I wasn't in a seatbelt… and poor Ryan was wedged on the floor between the back and front seat.

I prayed for an answer.

"Yea, though I walk through the valley of the shadow of death, I will fear no evil. For thou art with me."

The old psalm danced through my mind. And., I knew without any doubt, it was God.

As quick as it came, it left.

Yet… I had a sweet peace. As if, Jesus himself had just stepped into the car.

I've always heard stories about how Jesus is a present help in a time of trouble, and I've read about the miracles in the Bible… But I guess., this was the first time it became real to me. God was watching out for me. I was going to be okay.

"Excuse me, driver."

The driver screamed, loudly. He slammed on the breaks, honking the horn in the process. He turned around and I saw the beet-red, angry face of Avery Salazar.

Okay. Not who I was expecting. But okay.

"I was just wondering how much this taxi ride is going

to cost. I only have \$15."

"Chloe!" He screamed.

Ryan groaned.

"Sh. My man is resting."

I didn't expect what was coming next either. He reached for the pistol under his seat.

"You're going to shoot a helpless girl who doesn't even have a way to defend herself? That's low, Avery."

"I'll do what I want."

"That's at least a life time or two in prison."

"Shut up, Chloe."

"You said, you're not a murderer. Don't make yourself a liar and murderer in one night."

My heart was beating so loudly I could hear it in my ear drums.

"Oh God," I gasped.

Avery swung the pistol and it connected with my head.

4 THE RETURN

The door to the interrogation room clicked shut behind Detective Riley. He scanned the room. It wasn't distracting, yes, but it was all together boring.

Riley didn't care too much for the interrogation room; however, now that he was on the other side of the desk, it was tolerable. He'd spent his share of years where this young punk in sweats and a t-shirt sat. That's what made Riley the best, he knew how to get in the mind of the suspect.

Stupid kid doesn't know the end of the road he's traveling, thought Riley.

He shook his head and took a seat next to the kid.

"Hi, I'm Detective Riley. You must be Avery."

"How'd you ever guess."

Sarcasm must be how he deals with fear.

Riley spoke, "Football."

"Excuse me?"

"No. I change my mind. You're a basketball player."

"You must be crazy." Avery sounded disgusted, "I didn't come down to talk sports with you."

Cracking through the ice will be tough on this one.

"Ok, Avery. We'll break it down. I am a basketball player, and the guys are playing in 30 minutes. I'm sure you want to get out of here as quickly as possible," Riley checked his watch, "so we'll do this quick."

"Ok."

"Where were you last night?"

Avery averted eye contact. "At home."

"Really."

"Yes, I swear."

"Why don't you tell me where you really were."

Avery's sigh was almost unnoticeable. "I went to Jim's Fresh Market for something and went home and chilled."

"That's all you did."

"Yes."

"What kind of 'something' did you purchase?"

"Uhm. Alcohol?"

"I thought so."

This conversation was so familiar to Riley.

"You didn't go near Coffee Café?"

"No, Sir. Their coffee is too strong for me."

Riley reached for the remote on the end table between them.

"You're in luck, Salazar. I might get to the game tonight after all."

The monitor hanging on the wall came to life. The screen played a scene from Jim's Fresh Market. Two men came out and Riley changed the video to slow motion.

"Recognize that kid in the hoodie?"

"Yes, that's me."

Riley paused the scene which showed someone handing Avery a six pack of beer.

"Who is handing you the beer?"

"That's Gillis." Avery answered.

"Gillis, who?" Riley probed.

"Just Gillis."

Avery was unmovable. He wouldn't say anything without a further push.

"Okay. Do you want to tell me anything more about this Gillis man?"

"No."

"You're positive the two of you didn't go to Coffee Café afterwards?"

"Positive. I don't even drink coffee. That place is for preppy girls."

Detective Riley fidgeted with the remote until the screen showed a blurry image outside of Coffee Café. Avery and Gillis were walking out of the café.

Riley could almost hear Avery's heart drop.

"Ok, Avery. Level with me. Either, you're just a heartless criminal headed to federal prison, or someone put you up to it."

Avery squirmed in his seat.

"Avery, there are two sets of concerned parents out there, worried sick about their teenagers. Don't make them go into a panic attack. You saw the look on Mrs. Wyatt's face."

Suddenly Detective Riley's vision blurred, and Avery looked a lot like the detective who interviewed Riley those thirty some years ago. What did that detective do to help crack the ice of fear, "I know you're not a heartless crook. You're just a kid who got messed up in the wrong crowd."

Avery was speaking. Riley shook his head and tried to concentrate. Now was no time to live in the past.

"... even if I did, why should I tell you?"

"Because I know you're not a heartless crook. You just got in with the wrong crowd."

A quiet silence covered the room like a blanket of icy snow.

Finally, Avery spoke.

"His name is Andrew Gillis."

***

"Where am I?"

Ryan was coming to consciousness.

I watched him slowly stand up and walk around the shed which kept us captive. Moonlight filtered through a window and fell on his perplexed face. He walked to the door below the window and tried the handle.

"It's locked." He groaned.

I already knew that.

"What am I doing here?"

I figured I should say something before he found me. I didn't want to scare him.

"Same as me, I guess." He jumped at my words.

"Who else is here?" He was still confused.

"Just us, I think. Ryan, I'm so sorry," I said.

"What are you sorry about?"

"Avery... don't you remember?" I trailed off.

I watched the emotions play on his face: recognition, then anger.

"Messing with me is one thing, but Chloe. He hurt you." Ryan walked to me and brushed the loose hair from my face. "You have a black eye."

"It's my fault," I said.

"What? Why?"

"I wasn't going to say anything until I got permission. After tonight though, you deserve an explanation. I'm a spy," I quickly added, "But you seriously can't tell anyone."

"What are you talking about?"

"This was my first mission," I said, "I failed it, so I'm probably not anymore."

"Sounds dangerous."

"It wasn't supposed to be. We have certain safety precautions I had to take. I suppose I violated them when I didn't tell dad about Avery meeting us in the hallway. So, is there a way out of here? Our parents are going to kill us."

"I know, I'm probably grounded until I'm eighteen," Ryan said.

I limped over to the window and peered up. "There's a railroad spike half way up, could you give me a boost? I could try to pull myself up to the window."

"What's up with your foot? You're limping."

I ignored his question. "There's also a marijuana leaf painted on the door... this place gives me the creeps."

"How will you get down? If you jump you're going to hurt your ankle even worse."

"I think it's our only option, unless you want to stay here and starve. Or worse yet, wait for Avery to return. Don't forget that guy had a gun."

"But..." he started, "At least let me do the jumping."

"I can't give you a boost, quarterback, just get over here," I commanded with a laugh.

A few seconds later, I was up on the railroad stake. "This is higher than I thought; I can barely reach the window."

"Please be careful."

"Here goes." I grabbed the window and started pulling myself up. I thought I was going to fall for a second, but when I remembered the mysterious gun man, I managed to climb into the window cell.

"There you go," Ryan cheered, "you did it!"

"Ryan, it's a long way down. I don't know if I can do this."

"I'll catch you if you want to jump this way, we'll figure another way to get out of here."

"I like challenges."

"Chloe, are you okay? Chloe!"

A moment later I opened the door with a creak.

"I'm okay, there was a pile of hay where I jumped."

"What was locking the door?"

"A master lock," I replied, "apparently picking a lock isn't as hard as I thought."

"How did you do it?"

I smiled at him and held up a hair pin.

"Are you sure you're not related to Nancy Drew?"

"Maybe," I grinned.

Ryan came out of the shed. I took in our surroundings: trees, trees, and more trees. Ryan grumbled something about wishing he could see the North Star, and then began to look closely at a nearby tree.

"Ryan. Let's get out of here," I started walking away from the shed.

"Chloe. That way is south. I can tell from the moss growing on the tree."

"We don't even know which way Menominee is. What does it matter if we go north or south?" I asked.

None the less, I followed Ryan. We eventually came to a dirt road. The pinkish glow from the horizon cast grey shadows around us.

Our little country road ended into M-35 and we started walking toward town. The sun was beginning to peak over the bay waters when we saw the Menominee City Limits sign. Even though the morning winter frost was still kissing the surface of the earth, we were hot and worn out.

A pain shot up my leg from my ankle. I tried to cover it up with an awkward-looking skip; however, I think Ryan noticed because he suggested that we take a break.

He sat on the curb, waiting for me to join him.

I kicked a small rock that was on the road.

"Come on, Chloe. Take a break."

"Ryan. I'm not a baby. Let's keep going."

He reached for a hand up.

Yes, I won this one.

I slid my hand into his and waited for him to get up. We needed to get back to our parents. They were probably freaking out.

He gently tugged on my hand.

"Your ankle."

"Fine. But only for a second."

The road was deserted.

Ryan looked at me, "Well, that was definitely the first time I've ever met a gun man."

"Same."

It was almost an awkward silence. Almost because I'm pretty sure he could hear my heart beating.

Ryan looked up at the sky, as if searching for something to say. I looked at him from the corner of my eye; he really was cute.

Knock it off, Chloe. It's just Ryan.

"Thanks for letting me rest on the way out."

"What?" I asked.

"You shushed Salazar up, so I could rest."

I suddenly remembered what I said. *"Sh. My man is resting."*

I must have been blushing a pretty tomato shade of red, because Ryan was laughing.

"Okay quit. I can feel you judging me." I joined in on the laugh.

I heard the familiar whoosh of a vehicle passing. I looked up to see a red truck backing up.

Ryan dropped my hand and jumped up.

"That's my brother! Oh, Thank God we don't have to walk the rest of the way!"

David's truck was now parked in front of us and he was rolling down the passenger window.

"Where were you guys?" David yelled out the passenger window over his diesel motor. I followed Ryan to the truck, at a distance.

"Dad and mom are freaking out. And Chloe, your dad is searching frantically. He even has the FBI involved," David said.

"I'm sorry, but seriously, I can explain…" Ryan started. David cut him off.

"Just get in the truck, guys. I'll call dad and tell him you're okay." David grabbed his iPhone out of the cup holder.

Ryan opened the door; I climbed in the truck. I scooted in the middle seat to make room for Ryan.

David called his dad and explained what little he knew and promised to meet at their house.

"You had me worried, Munchkin," David said putting an arm around me, "By the way did I just see you two holding hands?"

"Uh, um, hmm… well you see…" I stammered.

"We were," Ryan said throwing a wink at me, "praying, well actually we were about to."

"Is that what we were doing?" I asked.

"Ah-ha. The perfect excuse to hold a beautiful girl's hand," David said kiddingly, "You know Chloe, you should watch this guy. He'll have you married to him before you know it."

"I'm pretty sure I'll know when I get married." I pulled my knees up on the seat and hugged them.

"So tell me kid, what happened? I thought you two eloped," David asked.

We told him what happened, or rather what parts we could remember and then re-told our parents when we got to the Ryan's home.

The parents were excited to see us, and relieved we were safe. Ryan hugged his parents, and humbly took all the attention he could get. Ryan's mom decided we all needed a late breakfast and went to the kitchen to make it. I followed her in to help.

"I'll not have the long-lost making the food; however, you can fix yourself a cup of coffee."

I stepped out of the kitchen. "Ryan, David, you want some coffee?"

They chorused their "yes".

"Brothers," Alexa, the oldest daughter of the Jones' family, walked into the living room, "this is your house. You should be getting Chloe coffee."

Before they could get up, she swatted them on the head with Positive Perspective, her favorite Bible college newsletter.

Alexa helped me carry the coffee in the living room. Since we'd all practically grew up together, I knew that Ryan loved a French vanilla latte, David like black coffee and Alexa – well she always tries something new.

For a while, no one really said much of anything. We just chilled in the living room by the warm crackling fire.

David broke the silence, "I just don't get it. Avery is just a kid. How could he kidnap two of you?"

I expected Ryan to answer; but, he avoided eye contact and turned a different shade of pink.

"He had a gun man." I shrugged. "He could have nabbed anyone."

"Scarey." Alexa mumbled.

"Uhm. Ryan?" I asked. His face was back to normal again. When I spoke, he broke the connection between his eyes and the floor.

"What's up?"

Man, you look exhausted.

I almost blurted out my thoughts. But instead, I spoke what I'd intended to before I met his blue eyes.

"Avery probably isn't happy about us escaping."

Saying them aloud opened a dam of fear in my heart.

"I know."

I heard something outside the window, and turned around to see a flashy car pulling up to the curb. A tall broad man stepped out. He wore a flashy suit, but I knew immediately he was the kind of guy who would rather wear sweats and throw the basketball on the court with the guys. He scanned the house, especially resting his eyes on the bushes which guarded the front door.

"Guys, look." My curiosity became contagious and we all watched him approach the house.

"Dude. He has his hand on hip like he's carrying." David spoke.

Dad answered the door and welcomed the mysterious man into the living room. Dad seemed totally chill with this man, but I wasn't so sure. He was scanning the room like he was waiting for a crazy man to come shoot the place up.

"Kids, this is Detective John Riley. He's from the local sheriff's department and would like to talk to you about your experience last night."

Don't you just love it how some adults will always call you a kid, even if you're driving and making plans for college? Oh well. I guess that's a dad thing.

"Hey," Ryan said.

Detective Riley must have taken that as an invitation, because he sat next to Ryan. He gently kicked Ryan's shoe. "I love the new Air-Justin's."

"Excuse me?" Ryan sounded just as confused as I was.

"Yeah. They're so much easier to play basketball in."

"Called it!" The words were out before I realized it.

"What?" Detective Riley had a kind smile and a laughable personality.

"Oh, I'm sorry. It's just that, I kind of thought you were the kind of guy who'd rather play basketball then wear a fancy suit. Oh, I'm sorry. Was that rude? I promise it wasn't meant to be."

"You're one-hundred percent accurate. You're a good judge of character."

"So, guys. Tell me, what happened last night?" He leaned back in his chair and looked comfortable.

We gave him our statement. It was a weird interview. Like, he wasn't writing anything down, just having a regular old conversation with us. He waited to ask questions until we finished.

"The man with Avery had a gun?"

"Yes, Sir," Ryan answered.

"So, Chloe, tell me again how the initial contact happened."

"Well, I was at the passenger side of the truck when I felt someone grab my jacket. And then, I guess instinctively I used a self-defense move."

"Now, was this your first time ever using a move as real self-defense?"

"Yes."

"I imagine it was different from practice. Your dad said you're a member of the Mid-County Girls' Martial Arts Club?"

"Yes," I said, "It's much different from practice. Breaking a board is easy. It doesn't hit back."

"Oh, don't forget about the marijuana leaf," Ryan said, "that way the shed can be identified."

Recognition washed over the detective. "We're on to the right trail. Ryan, could you show me and my guys where the shed is?"

"Sure thing!"

Mrs. Jones soon called us in the kitchen for breakfast. I didn't realize how hungry I was until she set the plate of scrambled eggs and bacon in front of me.

Detective Riley left shortly after breakfast with a promise for another visit.

***

I woke up with dread. Somewhere in my dreams, in the land of slumber, Avery was haunting me. I don't remember what was going on, but I guess a night like I had could give any girl nightmares.

Mom took the day off work to keep me home and baby me. I wasn't feeling well since I had spent all last night outside walking on my sprained ankle.

Mom declared today as pajama day. I sat in the recliner and cozied up in my warm red sweater. My hair was up in a messy bun and I was curled up in my zebra blanket and soaking in the warmth of the fire on this chilly spring morning. I closed my eyes and must have fell asleep, because the next thing I knew, I heard the doorbell ring. I jumped and started to get up.

"I'll get it, Honey." Mom said.

I pulled my zebra blanket over my eyes, praying it was just an elderly lady here to visit mom. I didn't want anybody seeing me like this, I probably looked ridiculous.

"Hey Chloe," Ryan said a few moments later walking in the living room. I froze under the blanket hoping he'd just assume I was sleeping or something.

"I know you're up. Your mom told me," he said.

I slowly peeked out from under my blanket and spotted him on the leather couch.

"I look like a wreck," I groaned.

"You do, but that's okay," he smiled at me, "I brought you something."

"Chocolate? Ryan, you're so sweet." I reached out for the box of chocolate on the side table between us.

"I'm really sorry for what happened last night. I blame myself. I should have protected you better, or at least have done something better," Ryan said.

"Oh Ry," I said, "he had a gun. There wasn't a thing anyone could have done. I was thankful you were there for me. I would have been stuck in a barn freezing if it weren't for you."

I slid my hair out of its messy bun and let it fall to one

side combing it with my fingers.

"Still if something would have happened to you, I never would have been able to forgive myself," he insisted.

We stared quietly at the fire crackling in the hearth. Its yellow and orange flames were gently enveloping the logs in a hug. I closed my eyes and breathed softly, I didn't realize how tired I was.

I woke up again with a start.

"Ryan?"

I looked around the room. I was alone. I didn't know what time it was, but my stomach was telling me it was time to eat again.

"Sweetie, is everything okay?" Mom appeared in the doorway.

"Was Ryan here earlier, or did I just dream it?" I asked slightly confused.

"He was here. How's your ankle doing?" She came over to inspect my ankle. With a frown, she looked up at me.

"You really should have made Ryan carry you. Walking on your ankle surely didn't help it."

"I think that would have been a little awkward. I can just imagine David's face if he saw Ryan carrying me." I laughed weakly at the idea. "What do you think of Ryan?"

"I like him. He seems to be a good friend for you," Mom answered slowly, "Why do you ask?"

"Oh, I don't know."

"Spill it." Mom said with a grin.

She sat on the couch next to me.

"Chocolate?" she asked. She twirled the box with her finger tip.

"Yeah, Ryan gave it to me." I said.

Mom raised an eyebrow. "Chloe."

"Oh, ok mom," I laughed, "you make it hard to be discreet."

"So?" Mom asked. She took my hand from across the coffee table and looked me in the eye.

"I don't know, it just seems that everything is changing. Another school year is going to be over, and then there's Ryan…" I drifted off, hoping mom would coax it out of me but she didn't. "I really, really like hanging out with him and he's seriously my best friend. But. I'm scared."

"Why?" Although Mom asked, I knew she had the answer. Moms have this way of knowing everything about their kids.

"Oh, I don't know. I just…. really admire him. When we were stuck in the shed, lost in the corn field and even walking forever on the road, he was so sweet. He was calm, cool, and knew what he was doing. The way he stood up for me when Avery came around…" I stopped. There was no way that Mom would understand what I was trying to say.

"You're not sure if you want to be boyfriend/girlfriend or just friends?" Mom said.

"That's exactly it! How did you know?"

"I was your age once too, baby. It's okay if you like Ryan. Guard your heart and pray about it. Remember, you're both still young - whom you fall in love with is likely to change because you're going to change."

"Thanks, Mom," I said. Mom gave me one of her comforting smiles and hugged me.

"I have to go make dinner, baby, do you need anything else?"

"No, thank you." I said.

***

That night as I sat in my bedroom, Faith called me to see how I was doing, or at least that's why she said she called me.

"I'm doing well. Mom has completely babied me." I said

laughing.

I stared at the mirror on my dresser. My brown hair was still wet from the shower I took a few minutes ago.

"Awe, that's sweet of her. You deserve it, bestie." She said.

"How are you?" I asked.

"Oh, all right I guess," she said. I knew she was a lot happier than she was letting on.

"Spill it, Faith. There's something you want to tell me." I said.

She laughed, and I could almost see the smile on her face.

"Okay, okay… I give," she said, "You know me too well. You're not going to believe this…" Faith dramatically paused.

"Just tell me."

"Chloe, calm yourself, it's just that Jordan took me to the sweetheart's banquet tonight."

"WHAT?!" I screamed into the phone speaker, "Jordan?"

"Yeah, I know. It's about time, I've seriously liked him since grade school."

"WHAT?" I yelled again.

This was news.

Faith and I always used to tell each other our crushes. She never told me about Jordan.

"So, are you guys dating?" I asked.

"I don't know, he is so cute." She paused, "Why weren't you and Ryan there? We all know you have a thing going on."

"He didn't ask me."

"Oh Chloe, I'm so sorry," she said, her voice dropped.

"No, it's okay. My mom wouldn't have ever let me out. She's still worried I'm going to catch a cold."

I was a little disappointed. My best friend had a date and I was just chilling at home.

***

Sunday afternoon Dad, Mom and I went out to lunch. We decided on Olive Garden. It was so delicious, and the setting of the restaurant was warm and inviting. We sat by a white chimney that trailed down to a warm fire. The walls were a warm cream colored and the tables and chairs were all wooden.

Our food came. We made light conversation over it.

Suddenly, the front door slammed making me jump. I looked up to see Miss Owens waddling through the door. Miss Owens is a sweet, old cat lady; I say that in the most respectful way.

She is notorious for two main things. First, she's notorious for spreading rumors, and secondly, match making. Although personally, she has never been able to find herself a catch, she has 'set up' at least half the couples in our town. I always get scared when she comes to visit us because I'm worried she'll send me on a blind date with some creep.

Miss Owens maneuvered her way through the tables, beelining it straight to our table. She slumped in the seat next to me.

Miss Owens has long black hair and brown eyes. She wears her glasses in the typical school teacher way, half way down the nose. Her style hasn't changed since high school and, that was forty years ago.

"Chloe Wyatt. I heard you were wreaking havoc on the town at wee hours with the minister's son. Do you have any idea, my dear, how terrible you make the poor family look?" Her eye had an accusing glean.

"But Miss Owen…" I tried to explain.

"When my sister, Mildred, told me she overheard the

grocery girl talking about Chloe's night, I was sure she was mistaken. I thought, 'Not sweet Chloe, why for goodness sakes, she wouldn't know how to!' I marched myself right up to the preacher's house and sweet Alexa confirmed it." She stared at me smugly, momentarily closing her mouth for the first time since she sat down. "I'll have you know Mr. and Mrs. Wyatt, I took great pains to come to you first."

As a waiter passed she called out to him, "Could I get some food? I'm starved." She turned to dad again and started talking, "I needed to know from her parents. WHAT WERE YOU THINKING?"

She had the attention of all attending the restaurant. I was so embarrassed. In this small town, news spreads fast. There will probably be a reporter from Channel 6 soon.

"What can I get you, ma'am?" The waiter asked as he took a pen and pad out of his black apron.

"Can't you see I'm busy? Come back in a second," Miss Owens said.

The confused waiter walked away.

"So seriously, Mrs. Wyatt, why did you let your daughter hang out with Ryan, doing who knows what to wreak havoc on the society of this town?"

"They didn't wreak anything..." Mom started but Miss Owens took over her sentence.

"... Yet. Little things lead to bigger things, you know that m'dear. It's disgraceful I tell you, and I'm very disappointed in all of you."

Miss Owens sat up straighter, then looked around the room, "Where is the stupid waiter, I'm ready to eat now. WAITER!"

I was trying hard to contain my laughter, but when I caught dad's gleaming eye, and the look on his face, I couldn't help but laugh.

Miss Owens glared at me. A moment later she swung her glare to the kitchen. "I'm starved."

"Eleanor," Mom said to Miss Owens, "Please calm down and listen to yourself, and us. Chloe and Ryan were not simply romping the town, they were kidnapped."

Mom continued to tell the whole story and Miss Owens was constantly picking her jaw up off the ground. She apologized profusely for jumping to conclusions.

It wasn't until after she promised to find me a 'suitable' boyfriend that she took her leave.

The poor waiter came back with a sympathetic smile. "I'm sorry about the wait."

He then realized Miss Owens was gone.

I think I saw him sigh in relief.

5 THE NEW KID

I sat in College Preparation with a smug smile. I finally had an occupation to pursue: I want to be a detective like Mr. Riley.

I only half listened as Mr. Grill droned on about applying for colleges. I was disappointed when he dismissed class without having open discussion about future career opportunities. I guess that's just my luck: when I have the opportunity, I don't have the words; when I have the words, I lack the opportunity.

I ended up in the back of the cafeteria line. My group had already staked claim on our table, so at least I didn't have to worry about eating in the hallways. The food variety was lacking by this time. The only thing that looked even okay-ish to eat was the cold macaroni and cheese.

The conversation at our table was lacking. I guess, more appropriately, I should say it was non-existent. I noticed the new kid right away. He was lanky and had sandy-blonde hair.

Everyone knows how much I hate awkward silences. I'd rather be awkward then bear through an awkward silence.

"Hey guys," I smiled. They were still mute.

I sat down, across from the sandy-blonde haired new kid.

"I'm Chloe."

Faith came up behind me, food tray in hand. She slid behind me, so she could sit next to Jordan. His eyes lit up and he side-hugged her gently.

"Hey, babe," Faith said.

I almost vomited. What was going on here? Jordan is a lot of things: an amazing line runner and state champion in track - but he isn't babe.

Well, I guess there's somebody for everybody.

I slid in across from the new kid. I hesitantly looked at the group waiting for someone to introduce him. When nobody did, I spoke.

"Hey, I'm Chloe. Are you new here?"

"Yeah."

"Oh okay, well, welcome to our school! It's cool for the most part. Except the macaroni and cheese is pitiful." I mocked a pout, hoping to crack a smile from this mysterious kid.

"Do you want some French fries?" Ethan asked and pushed them toward me, "I'll never eat these."

The white plate was covered with sizzling fries, salted to perfection.

Be still. My beating heart.

"Oh my gosh, can I? You'll be like, my best friend!"

"Have them all if you want," he grinned and threw a wink in my direction. "My name is Ethan by the way."

Ryan cleared his throat. I glanced at him. His face was the same shade as his flushed-red plaid shirt. With his right hand he brush his brown hair out of his eyes.

"Excuse me," he was talking to Ethan, but looking at me.

Ethan slid out of the booth and Ryan followed.

"Does anybody need anything while I'm up?" Ryan was looking at me again.

"Can you get me some more coke?" I slid my tall red coke glass to the edge of the table.

In one fluent motion, Ethan swiped the cup; Ryan's hand missing by milliseconds.

"Oh, I'll get it," Ethan said, "I'm headed up anyways."

"I can get it," Ryan said as he tried to grab the cup out of Ethan's hand. It just resulted in the cup cracking on the ground with an echoing crash.

Ethan bent down and took the cup in his hand. "I need more soda anyway. You're going to the coffee station."

Ryan mumbled, "Sorry, man."

I watched Ethan walk to the soda fountain and get me a new cup. I was thankful for his consideration, otherwise, I'd be leaking soda all over my new outfit.

**

The door of Mrs. Anderson's English class closed, rather loudly, behind me.

"Faith, save me!" I fell in step with my best friend in the noisy hallway. Students were slamming their lockers and racing to the front entrance like prisoners who were just released.

"From whom, exactly, am I saving you?"

"Boys," I rolled my eyes.

"Oh please, Chloe, even if I could I wouldn't."

We passed through the doors to the commons. It was quieter here, and much easier to talk

Faith continued, "You're the one who, when we played Barbie's, always stole Ken. Now, even if you don't want him, you're stuck with him."

I glared at my best friend. I knew she was teasing; but, it didn't take my frustration away.

Ryan has been acting weird since Ethan showed up. Like, for example, in English class we were supposed to be studying Romeo and Juliet. Ryan kept making a point to be my study partner. Almost as if he was jealous Ethan was showing me attention. It's so annoying.

"Everybody always says, and to an extent I agree, that girls are dramatic. I'd like to proclaim from the highest point," I paused and impulsively jumped up on the lunch table, "for all to hear that drama knows no gender. Boys and girls alike are huge drama queens. Or kings, I guess it'd be. To prove my hypothesis, I present to you-" I was ready to tell the whole story. Spill out the beans, so to speak. I knew Faith could give me some sound advice.

"Chloe?" Ethan interrupted walking through the big double doors at the end of the room. He looked around the deserted cafeteria and then back at me.

"Yes?"

"What are you doing?

"I'm annoyed."

"So, when you're annoyed you climb on top of tables and declare heart felt messages," Ethan said clearly amused, "duly noted."

"Oh, stop making fun and help the lady down." I said dramatically.

I don't know what I expected, maybe a hand down or him just to laugh at me and tell me to get lost. I didn't expect what happened. In one seemingly effortless motion, Ethan swept me off my feet into his arms.

"Put me down!"

He grinned at me. I needed to get my feet on solid ground. *Now.*

"And what if I don't?" He gently set me on my feet and steadied me.

I did a quick survey of the cafeteria, hoping nobody was watching. Thankfully, Faith, though doubled over laughing, was the only witness.

A throat cleared in the entry. I looked up and locked eyes with Ryan. He looked so confused; shook his head and walked away.

I ran out of the cafeteria, leaving a bewildered Ethan. Faith stopped laughing, "Chloe. Chloe! Are you okay?"

She was running after me. All I could think about was Ryan.

I caught up with him near his truck. He reached to open the door and I slammed my back against it, completely out of breath.

"No. You. Don't. Ryan Jones."

"What do you want?" Ryan's voice was so pouty, I could hear I-am-a-two-year-old soaked in every word.

"That. Was an accident. Just so you know." I nervously looked into his beautiful brown eyes.

"It's okay, Chloe. You like the new kid. That's fine. I'm happy for you." He wasn't happy for me or anyone. He was mad. His voice, body language and red face gave it away.

I rolled my eyes. "You. Are so dense."

"Excuse me?"

I angrily began to walk away.

"Chloe. You can't just walk up to me and insult me for no reason."

"Yea?" I turned around, trying in vain to get my emotions concealed. I hate how easily I cry.

He gestured in frustration and opened his truck door.

"Okay. Let me put it a different way. Why did you just walk up and insult me?"

"Because you are dense." I walked away feeling for the second time again that day that when I had the opportunity, I lacked the words.

He slammed his truck door and started his engine. Something shifted in me. I knew I liked Ryan, but I lacked the courage to tell him. I was sure he was going to laugh at me, friendzone me and call me immature. I was just the girl next door, in his mind.

His brake lights flashed, and I knew I had to do something. I was not letting my best friend, and biggest crush I've ever had, leave me behind to smell the goodbye of his diesel truck exhaust.

I ran to the driver's door and stepped on the running board.

I slammed my fist on the window until he rolled it down. His eyes almost looked watery. Or maybe I was mistaken, because men don't cry. *Right. Of course they cry. He was.*

Now that the time came, I didn't have the words. I didn't know how to tell him how I felt. I opened my mouth, and nothing came out.

I swallowed hard.

"I-," my voice was small, "I called you dense. Because. Ryan," now I was the one gesturing in frustration, "I think. I love you."

6 DREAM GIRL

Wednesday evening Mom and I were sitting on the white wicker front porch swing, enjoying the fresh air.

"You-who, Mrs. Wyatt!" Miss Owens called from the street interrupting our peaceful time.

Mom waved at the woman leaning against our white picket fence. "Oh Miss Owens! How nice of you to stop by. Do you have a minute to visit?"

Mom and Miss Owens have a very interesting friendship. They're complete opposites, yet they can sit for hours and visit.

"Definitely!" She was already walking up the brick pathway to the porch. She waddled up the front steps and sank into a lawn chair.

"Chloe," Miss Owens said, "be a dear and get me a cup of tea."

I nodded and stood up.

"Honey," Mom sent me a sympathetic smile, "there's a new batch of sun tea on the back porch."

I heard Miss Owens chatter about the latest gossip in town as I slipped into the house.

I found the sun tea and poured a glass for mom and Miss Owens. I grabbed a soda for myself and headed back to the porch. I opened the door. Miss Owens was speaking in a hushed, rushed voice.

"So, I did a little digging around for you, because I just felt so horrible for accusing Chloe the other day in the restaurant. I found out that Avery disappeared after a little interrogation with some Mr. Riley man. His mom thinks he's been coming by in the middle of the night and stealing food and money."

Her voice showed intense interest, "She's getting slightly annoyed and probably going to tell the police soon. She just feel so bad because Avery is her only son. For him to end up in juvenile detention again would just be too much.

"She feels like a horrible mom because of what happened. I agree with her. Well, when I said that, she promptly threw me out. Can you imagine that? All I did was agree with what she was saying and she tossed me to the street like I was a stray orphan. Thanks for the tea, by the way, Chloe."

Miss Owens spoke as if everything she had to say needed to come out in the same breath.

I stayed on the porch listening to Miss Owens drone on for the rest of that evening. My thoughts were preoccupied trying to figure out where Avery could be staying, and what The Lions were up to.

Dad or the agency hadn't talked to me about my mission since I botched it up. Honestly, for a while, I tried not to think about it. But now, my curiosity was running rapid. I wondered… if I finished the mission, would the agency consider accepting me back on the team?

I remembered the date: February 29. What was happening then? That was only 10 days away.

I decided to do a little snooping. For the first time in all my sixteen years, I snuck out. From my black shoes to my black hoodie that my hair was tucked into – I was as dark as night.

The back door quietly shut behind me, closing off the light from the house. The moon, though hidden behind clouds, illuminated the sidewalk as I neared the end of Douglas Street.

I'd only been to Avery's trailer park once. I'd been selling Girl Scout cookies in grade school. I remembered, Avery opened the door and roared something about not supporting cookie fatties. I'd been afraid to return and always avoided the end of Douglas Street at all costs.

Now, here I was sneaking around at eleven-thirty in the dark.

I slowed my pace when I arrived at their neighbor's trailer. I decided to sneak behind the oak trees in the front. From there, I'd be able to get to the lilac bushes on the side of the house. Then I could see the front and back door.

I crouched in the lilac bush and peered between the branches. I began to second guess coming here. What was I going to do if I saw Avery, or worse yet, what if he saw me?

A light flickered on in the basement; I realized it was too late to turn around now. I just had to know if Avery was still around.

The light stayed on for a few minutes and then turned off. I could see through one of the first level windows that someone was walking around with a flash light. I was intensely interested in what was going on in the house.

A twig snapped next to me. Reeling around, I saw a figure kneeling inches away. Heart racing, a grip tightened on my forearm and a hand slid over my mouth.

This was it. I was going to die.

Why didn't I stay home like the good girl I, usually, was?

Fear swallowed my muffled scream. Regret washed over me like the slippery sweat that slid down the side of my face.

"It's just me," a low whisper in my ear.

"Ethan," I breathed. Instantly, I relaxed. "What are you doing here?"

"I'll explain later," his voice matched my hushed-whisper, "We need to be quiet. He will be coming out soon."

"And then what?"

"Usually I'd follow him," I thought I detected a slight annoyance in his words, "But you're here."

Before I could spout off that he was also ruining my plans, the back door shut.

Avery walked out.

A moment later a crying toddler came running after him, slamming the door behind.

"Avery, I saw you. Come home Avery, I miss you!" she cried.

She was standing in a white night gown, her golden curls framed her child-like face.

Avery ran back to her, reassuring her he'd come back and that everything would be all right. I could tell this girl, who I assumed to be his little sister, held a soft spot in Avery's heart.

Finally, he convinced her to go back in the house and he disappeared in the woods.

I could now interrogate the new kid, "What are you doing here?"

His response was annoyingly protective, "I think I need to get you home. It's not safe here."

Offended, I retorted, "I'm fully capable of taking care of myself."

"And what if it would have been Avery who spotted you here instead of me?"

"I- don't know. But you don't need to mother me."

"Fair enough," he shrugged, "but I think we both agree it's time to go home."

"Whatever." I grumbled.

He walked with me all the way home.

At the back door, I realized I left my key and it was locked. Ethan was already disappearing in the shadows.

I called after him. He stopped and I jogged to his side.

"Since you're here, would you mind giving me a boost?

"What?"

"Yeah," I said, "I just need to reach the porch roof. I can get it from there."

"You mean your parents don't know you're out this late?"

"You obviously don't know my parents, they don't let me out after nine o'clock."

"I didn't figure they sent you on a mission to spy on Avery."

He chose the word mission, like he knew I'd already been on one?

I climbed up on the roof under my window and then into my room. I didn't realize the intensity of my stupidity until my window was locked shut.

Avery's friend already pulled a gun once, he could have done it again tonight. I could have died over this stupid mission. I leaned against the windowsill peering into the darkened sky. I promised myself I'd be more careful next time.

***

The next day at school our principal called a school-wide meeting in our first period. We met in the lecture hall, the only room big enough to hold all the students.

The room was full of teenagers chattering; the echo of their voices made it seem like there were more kids than our number.

One of the teachers stepped from behind the red

curtain and made his way to the center of the stage.

"Attention students." He said, after about three attempts to quiet the room he finally silenced the crowd.

"Our principal has something very important to talk to us about. We'd appreciate it if you'd zip your lips and open your ears. No more talking is allowed until after Mr. Stevens is done speaking."

A dull roar of whispers waved over the room.

"Students," the teacher said sternly, "quiet."

The room was silent again.

"Mr. Stevens, please come to the podium."

The teacher walked off stage and principal Stevens took his place.

"Students, I appreciate your attentiveness." He scanned the crowd, "I have a very important issue to discuss with you.

"I believe in tolerance; however, I also believe in intolerance. I will not tolerate spray paint on the school walls, drugs in the classroom, teachers getting threatened, or students getting bullied.

"We have rules. These rules protect students and provide a save environment for education. These rules will be respected, or there will be consequences."

He ended his speech and few applauded. Another teacher went up and dismissed us to our classes.

I slipped out of the room while another teacher was going over announcements. On my way to the restroom, I thought I heard someone say my name in the cafeteria. I stopped and leaned against the closed door.

"She was there last night, wasn't she?" It sounded like Avery.

"No," The quiet, persuasive voice belonged to Ethan.

"It was bad enough to have you snooping on me, but I won't tolerate that girl double crossing me. Again."

"Don't worry Salazar, she's too chicken to try anything else."

I clenched my teeth.

What did he mean, I was chicken?! I'll show him who's chicken!

Was Ethan working with Avery?

"Okay, well she'd better stay away. I've kidnapped her once and I'm not afraid to take care of her again. Her and that preacher boy are always getting in the way."

"Yeah, he is annoying." Ethan agreed.

I could not believe what I was hearing.

"Oh, I'm meeting with Andrew Gillis today," Avery bragged, "He says he needs a little more help, and he's willing to pay big time. I'll bring the stuff tonight."

Andrew Gillis! I finally had a name. Was he the outside contact or the gunman?

Ethan was talking again. "I thought we were done working with him. It's too dangerous."

"Where do you think I've been staying this whole time?" Avery hissed, "and if you're too chicken, you're welcome to back out; but, I might just forget to pay you."

"You promised! And you know I need this money." Ethan was pathetically begging.

"Well, I guess you have to work for me. That little goody two-shoe has to work for me too, I've got some dirt on her."

"You should really leave the girl out of this. What good is she?" I don't know if Ethan was protecting me, or just had a really low opinion of me.

I'll show him!

"Oh, I don't know. I just remembered my dad said it's always good to have a little dirt on people."

"Man, you need to get out of here. I think the meeting is over."

"Yes, give me a ride out of this place." Avery's voice

again, "Those were lofty words the principal said, weren't they? Too bad he can't do anything about us."

His villain laugh echoed into the hall. Their footsteps approached the door.

Avery spoke again. "We're nine days away from the February 29 deal. We can't botch this."

So… Ethan was working with Avery. But why was he following him, was he lying to me? Why would he care if Avery found me?

I tiptoed away from the door.

For the remaining of the day, I was distracted by the many unanswered questions swarming in my mind. Who is Andrew Gillis? and what kind of stuff is he willing to pay for? Drug dealing is the first thing that came to mind.

Not exactly comforting.

I was coming out of the girl's locker room when I spotted Ethan. I decided to play it cool.

"Hey Ethan."

He turned around.

"What's up, Chloe?" He looked perfectly innocent.

"I was just wondering if you wanted to catch up after school. Coffee Corner has good coffee."

I smiled nonchalantly, inwardly begging him to take the bait. I figured if I spend time with Ethan I might be able to figure out what his relationship with Avery was.

"Awe, isn't that the sweetest thing ever. I'll meet you in the common area."

"After the bell rings!" I called out.

"Oh hey. And, Chloe?"

"Yes?"

"They're still trying to clean your footprints off the table. So maybe you could refrain from being annoyed."

I glared at him.

I was enjoying this whole undercover work. If I figure anything out, the Agency would request another mission from me. I was sure.

I met up with Ethan and we walked to Coffee Corner.

It was packed with kids coming out of school. I kept glancing over my shoulder.

The only person I didn't want seeing me here with him was Ryan. And., maybe Avery.

I hadn't seen Ryan, beside briefly in class, since I confessed my quote-unquote love for him. Feeling rather ridiculous, I tried to brush away any thoughts of him.

However, he was there. Like a constant plague.

I'm not sure how I expected him to react. But driving away wasn't it. Even if he didn't like me back in "that way", just driving away still isn't the way best friends treat each other.

Shoulda' left him in the friendzone.

Once we were seated I casually waited for Ethan to start a conversation.

"So, I assume you know I got kicked out of my old school."

"I didn't know."

"It wasn't really my fault."

I silently waited for him to continue.

"Someone got blackmail on me and forced me into working for them. I wish I would have just stood up to her, because what she was making me do was worse than what I actually did."

"She?" I asked.

"Her name was Ashley Ground. We dated for a while."

Abruptly, I set my glass down; it teetered on the table top. "Ashley Ground? You dated, Ashley?"

"Do you know her?" He asked looking at me intensely.

"Yeah, she used to date Avery Salazar."

"Oh, he must have been the guy she dumped me for."

Ethan was acting like he didn't even know Avery.

I was beginning to wonder if it really was Avery and Ethan talking in the cafeteria.

"Oh, I was wondering… why were you at Avery's last night, and why do you follow him?" My blunt comment didn't come out as casual as I'd envisioned.

He took a sip of his coffee, "Is that Avery's house?"

"Yes."

He took another slow sip and poured some sweetener in his spoon; taking his time dropping the substitute for sugar his steaming coffee.

Come on, Ethan. Stop delaying. Tell me.

Finally, he spoke. "Why were you there?"

"Well I assume you know about Ryan and me getting kidnapped. Channel 6 did a news story on it."

I was soon telling him the whole story; his gaze was intensely focused on mine.

Abruptly, I remembered he never answered my question.

When I pointed it out, he just said, "Oh yeah, well I guess my story is for another time. I need to head to work."

I realized he wasn't planning on talking to me about it.

"I'll see you later, Chloe. Thanks for talking." He smiled and walked up to the front counter.

***

That night I was sitting in some bushes opposite of where Ethan found me the other night. My intention was to follow Ethan, who was supposedly following Avery.

We'd have a regular game of follow the leader in session.

I was startled when I heard a little voice called out the door.

"Avery?"

His little sister.

Her cute little face was sticking out from the door way;

her golden curls dangled in front of her blue eyes.

She walked outside, wearing the same white pajamas. She stood still for a minute, and then began to chase a firefly; her bare feet pattered against the wet grass.

The bothersome bug flew towards me and I began to worry she would find me. I didn't move, but when the bug flew right into the bush I knew the little girl would see me.

It landed on my leg. Carefully, I caught it and stepped out of the bush.

"Who are you?" she asked in a frightened panic.

"Don't be scared," I tried to keep my voice low and assuring, "I caught your bug."

She slowly came to me and I moved it from my hand to hers.

"Thank you, nice lady," she looked up at me, "you're really beautiful."

I looked around. I had to get out of here. She was waiting for me to respond, so I did. "Thanks."

"What's your name?"

"I'm Chloe." After the words escaped my mouth I realized how stupid I'd just been. Of course, she would tell Avery I was here.

"I'm Gracie. Are you a dream lady?"

"I might be." I said, "Why don't you go back to bed?"

"I'm waiting for my big brother. He doesn't like anyone but me. He's the only one I have left." She smiled, jerking her thumb to herself. "How did you get here, dream lady?"

"You can't tell anyone about dream ladies, you know, otherwise they'll never come back." I said, thinking quickly.

"You'll come back?" She asked eagerly.

"Yes, one day. Dream ladies always come back. I have to go now."

"Bye, dream lady," Grace said waving, "I won't tell anyone because I want you to come back."

I blew her a kiss and left in the opposite direction of my home. Feeling a little gutsy I doubled back and hid in another bush.

"Hey, dream girl," a voice whispered next to me.

I jumped. I turned to my left and saw Ethan.

"You again?" I asked.

"You bet. You're ruining my plans again."

"Well, you're ruining mine. You obviously know this is Avery's house, Ethan. What are you up to?"

The front door slammed before he could answer. Gracie came out again.

"Avery." She called softly.

Her only answer was the disappointed blowing of the wind. She sat on the door step, folded her arms, and sank her head into them.

Soft sobs escaped her lips, and my heart hurt for her.

I longed to go comfort her, but I hesitated. What if Avery came back and saw me?

In the school, when I overheard Ethan and Avery talking, he said that he'd already taken care of me once and wasn't afraid to do it again.

She looked up at the bush where she saw me last.

"I lied dream lady, now I don't have nobody but you."

She looked up at the sky; tears had swollen her cheeks.

"That's it." I gritted through my teeth.

I stood up and was about the break through the branches.

Ethan placed a hand on my shoulder.

"Where do you think you're going?" He hissed.

"Gracie. She needs me."

"You can't. Avery might see you and who knows what he'll do to you. He's already pulled a gun on you, he might do it again you know. I need you to work as a team."

I didn't listen to reason, though I should have. I jerked

away from Ethan and did my best to impersonate a dream lady's walk

I've never seen a dream lady, in fact before today I didn't even know what a dream lady was. I guess she is just a lady who lives in a dream.

"Hello Gracie." I said in a dreamy voice.

"Dream lady!" She ran to me and hugged me.

"I am all alone now! Avery didn't come home tonight." She sobbed in my arms.

"It's okay. Avery still loves you."

I hoped what I was saying was true, and from what I saw the other night, I thought it was safe to say.

"I- I know. It's just that he said he would come back. He said Daddy will come home, and Mom will stop crying and we'll be a happy family like the one I saw on TV."

"Well, Avery must know what he's talking about."

"I wish you could stay forever, dream lady."

"I can't, Gracie, but maybe someday I can return in another dream," I said pulling away from her, "Now, go back in bed."

She smiled at me and I returned the smile.

I ran to the street and then through a neighbor's yard to the next street. I made my way home, climbed up the trellis by my window and snuck in the window.

***

"Hey Chloe." Ryan said.

I was sitting at our usual seat in the cafeteria.

"Hey Ryan." I looked up groggily at him.

"I brought you a coffee. You look pretty tired." He smiled sweetly at me and my heart did one of those flip-flop things.

Wait, what was wrong with me, this is only Ryan. I couldn't help remembering how he'd just backed up and left after I'd confessed my "love" toward him. I chided myself for being so awkward. Ryan just wanted to be friends. Though the atmosphere was presently awkward, I decided to not let it stay awkward. I valued Ryan's friendship too much.

"I am tired. I didn't sleep well last night." I admitted.

He set the cup of coffee in front of me and sat down.

"Where's everyone else?" I asked.

"They're still getting food."

"It seems like we haven't talked forever." I stated the obvious.

"I know."

It was silent for a moment, but not an awkward silence, so I didn't feel the need to say anything.

"Chloe, about the other day," Ryan started, "were you being serious?"

I looked away. "Ryan, it's okay. Don't worry about that. You know I talk quicker than I think."

Ryan sighed. "I am a dense idiot."

I laughed lightly. "No. I'm the idiot."

Ryan glance around the cafeteria, and brought his gaze back to me.

"Chloe. I've liked you since the day you glued my suit in Sunday school when we were three-years old. And, remember that middle school dance I was too shy to invite you to? It's the time you came bursting through those doors, tripped on your high heel shoe and landed at my feet." He laughed.

I kicked him from under the table. "Ok, Jones. Shut it." I laughed.

"I just wanted to say, I'm sorry for acting like such an idiot and for being so dense."

I smiled. "There's nothing to forgive."

"Will you – be my girl?"

7 IDENTIFIED

I went to the mall after school, it was buzzing with activity. Music blared, sales people were talking to those who passed, and a few guys in white shirts and dress pants were handing out church cards. I walked to the beat of the catchy tune on the radio, carrying my few shopping bags.

It'd proved to be a pretty successful shopping day, because I still had money left over for a late dinner.

I went into Appleburger and took a seat, setting my bags down on the floor next to me.

Sometimes dining by yourself is boring, but today I enjoyed the time alone. It offered time to think; and today I had a lot to think about.

First, there was my new relationship with Ryan. It was all new.

I also thought about the date Feb 29, it was only three days away. I was beginning to accept my failure as a spy.

When my food came, I noticed her. She was standing at the entry holding a man's hand; her blonde little curls neatly combed out.

They were too far away for me to hear their voices, but I knew without any doubt, it was Gracie.

They followed the waiter to a table that was too close

for comfort. I tried to melt into my booth.

"Avery, I don't like your old man get up." She poked at his mustache and it fell off. Avery quickly stuck the fake mustache back on his face.

"Hush Gracie. Remember, you're supposed to call me Jesse."

"But you're not Jesse," she loudly insisted, "you're Avery."

"Shush, baby girl." Avery put a finger to his lips.

"I got to go to the bathroom, Avery - I mean Jesse."

"You see that door with the girl in the skirt? That's the one." He pointed past me toward the back wall.

If Gracie kept her eyes straight, she wouldn't see me.

"But, I'm wearing pants." She said looking down at her legs.

"It's okay Gracie."

She gave him a pout and then started walking to the bathroom. I relaxed against the booth when she passed without noticing me.

At the bathroom she pondered the two doors: pants and a skirt. A man briskly walked by her and went into the men's room. She decided on the one with the dress.

I kept my head down, pretending to intensely study my purse.

The bathroom door banged again, and she came out humming and skipping.

She appeared to not notice I was there and passed me.

She did a double take.

She stopped at the end of my table and stared at me.

"Are you, the dream lady?" She whispered.

"Avery is going to notice you here with me, and then I can't come back. Remember you can't tell anyone?" I peeked over my menu.

"Gracie." Avery called her from his table.

"Gracie, go back now." I said seriously.

"But, Avery… he won't make you go away. I think he'd like to meet you. He needs a dream lady. He doesn't believe in dream ladies, but he will when he meets you." She said smiling.

"I'm not his dream lady," I said thinking fast, "I'm just a normal girl around him."

"Oh, I see. Well I think he wants to meet you. You're really pretty."

I heard footsteps and began to panic.

"Gracie, come here," Avery said.

I could tell he was approaching. I slid into my hoodie, pulled the hood up and hid my whole face in the menu.

"I don't want to."

"Gracie, if you don't listen you can't come next time," he warned.

I sensed him looking at me. I willed Gracie to go away, but she didn't. Instead she sat down in the seat across from me.

"Gracie." Avery said sternly.

"I don't want to go with you. I like her."

"I'm really sorry about this." I heard Avery sit down next to Gracie.

I kept my head in my menu and mumbled something.

"I don't want to go." Gracie repeated.

"Gracie, you have to."

"I'm not leaving this bench until I can order dessert off her menu."

I heard Avery stand up and I assumed he took a menu from the table next to him.

"No! I want her menu." Gracie stood up on the bench, snatched my menu and let it crash on the table; leaving me with absolutely no cover.

"You." Avery said as he immediately recognized me.

"Is there a problem?" I asked, trying to sound casual and annoyed. Inside, my heart was pounding with fear.

"Yeah, you're my problem. You never seem to go away, do you?"

"I'm simply eating dinner at the mall." I explained, trying to stay calm.

"A likely story, you're spying on me. Again." Avery gritted his teeth.

"I'm not. I was here first."

"I want a pumpkin pie and a cheese cake, Avery – I mean Jesse," Gracie leaned on the table between us and looked up at him, "can I please have a pumpkin pie and cheese cake?"

She was oblivious to what was going on between us.

"Hang on, Gracie." Avery said.

"I knew you'd think my dream lady was pretty!" Gracie said clapping her chubby hands together.

"She's not dream lady. Her name is Chloe, and she is trouble."

"No," She pouted, "she is dream lady. She helped me the night you didn't come home."

He glared at me.

"So, I was right. You were there." Avery said, his eyes piercing into mine.

I stared at him, thinking of what to say. "What are you doing with Andrew Gillis?"

Avery snickered, "As if I'd tell you, as if I really could."

"You could you know. There's always the option of coming clean and telling me what's going on."

"You goody-two-shoes really know it all don't you? Then what would happen to her," he said jerking his head at Gracie, "I've done my best to shelter her from my dad's problems, my mom doesn't even try. I'm all she's got left. I can't 'come clean' and land in juvenile detention."

"What have you done?"

"It wasn't supposed to be anything serious, just a few messages and deliveries. I was getting paid big, and I really needed it. It's what Gracie and I live off. Then he got more demanding."

"Deliveries?"

"He didn't outright say they were drugs, but it was easy to assume."

I silently wait for him to continue.

"I got scared when I found out you were an agent. I had no idea what I was going to do with you and Ryan in the shed."

"Andrew was the man with the gun?" I asked.

"Yes. He told me to take care of you guys."

"Well," I said dryly, "thank you for sparing my life."

The hint of a smile played on his lips, "I'm not a murderer. I just got messed up with the wrong people. I'd never kill anyone."

"I believe you," I paused, wondering how much information I could pull from Avery, "What's the deal with February 29th?"

Fear washed over his face. "I – won't tell you."

"Avery. If it's true, you just got messed up with the wrong people, then come clean. Help the authorities, they'll probably be easier on you."

"I've told you too much already." Avery's guard was back up again. "If you tell a soul, Chloe, you'll regret it."

"Turn yourself in, Avery." I coaxed.

He left the restaurant without a word.

8 THE NEW BEGINNING

I struggled the whole ride home whether to tell dad, or just forget that I ever saw Avery.

I decided to talk to dad; which is, exactly what I did when I got home.

He obviously found out I was sneaking out, because Gracie recognized me. He made me promise not to sneak out anymore. "It's too dangerous now," he said.

I agreed. I didn't like seeing him so worked up.

The next day, Ethan and I sat on the gym bleachers watching Ryan, Christian and Jordan throw the ball around the school's gym. Their squeaking shoes echoed along with their shouts.

"I'm done sneaking out." I said.

Ethan raised an eye brow. "Oh really?"

"Yeah, dad found out."

"That's the worst."

I nodded. "Where are your parents?"

Ethan got a faraway look in his eye. "My mom left when I was a baby, and my dad works in the service. I'm living with my uncle."

"Oh," I said, "I'm sorry about your mom."

"In some ways, my dad was more than any mother could

be to me. In other situations, it just wasn't the same."

"How long have you lived in Menominee?" I asked.

"A few months. My dad thought it would be good for me."

Ethan looked uncomfortable with the conversation. I realized this is the first time he talked about himself.

***

Dad was gone again when I got home. Mom wouldn't come right out and tell me. I knew he was gone with the sheriff to Andrew Gillis' house. Mom's face bore the worry she felt for her husband.

Dad didn't come home until eleven that night. He didn't come home alone. Behind him stood Detective Riley, the same man who was at the Jones' the morning after we were kidnapped.

They walked to the kitchen. Dad started making coffee.

I slowly shadowed them into the kitchen and eased into a conversation. "I'm so glad you're okay. How did it go?"

Dad's words were kind, but stern, "It's confidential, Chloe."

"Nathan, she's part of this mission, I think you should tell her."

I inwardly thanked God for the detective.

Dad sighed.

"We arrived at Andrew Gillis' house and found what we expected; marijuana. Our dogs found drugs all around the property; in the house, garage, and barn. Avery was camped out in the basement. He was more scared than a lost puppy dog. We also found that black convertible you told us about. Apparently, that's Gillis' getaway car."

Mr. Riley picked up where dad left off. "Your dad introduced himself to Avery; he promised to tell us everything - he just had to speak to you first."

"So, where is he?" I asked.

"Avery is at the station." Dad answered.

I stood up. "Let's go!"

"No." Dad spoke the words with determination.

"Dad I need to."

Dad seemed to be weighing it out. With everything in me, I willed him to say yes. I knew I couldn't go against what he said as final word – but I also knew I had to speak with Avery.

I walked to the foyer, grabbing my jacket and keys.

"Chloe," he said, "I… okay."

***

Avery was sitting in the witness room of the Menominee City Police Station. His head perked up when I walked through the door.

I made my way to him; he stood as I approached. We stared at each other for a while; it was like we were having a conversation with our eyes. His eyes begged me to understand his silent plea.

"You have it all, everything I've ever wanted." His words were emotionless.

"Avery," I started, but he cut me off.

"All I ever wanted in life was for my dad to care."

"I'm so sorry, Avery."

He sat down and slammed his fist on the chair's arm. Emotion now played thickly through his words, "I don't want your sympathy. I just want you to appreciate what you have. Your dad, he saved me. He showed me I could get help. I was sitting there, in the basement of a man who had so many promises; I'd get my college paid for and my little sister would be safe. It was perfect. I'd just deal a few drugs for him in school and he'd pay me big time. The same man who promised so much, left me penniless and headed to jail, alone."

"Avery…"

"I don't want your sympathy. I want your promises."

"My promises?" I asked.

"You're a good girl, Chloe. I knew as much the night we met in the parking lot behind the school. You're gorgeous. You're smart - everything a guy could ask for. Don't ever settle, and don't get messed up like I did."

"I promise."

"That, and promise me you'll visit Gracie."

"I promise."

He leaned back in his seat, looking like a weight rolled off his shoulders.

A moment later, I made eye contact with him. "Avery, you're not a bad guy."

He huffed sarcastically, as if he wanted to believe me, but inwardly, he couldn't.

"I'm serious. It doesn't matter how messed up you've gotten in this deal. God has always been there – waiting for you. He loves you. He's ready to forgive you and give you a new life."

"Why would God want to forgive me? Why would He care? Nobody else has."

"Because He loves you, Avery." I said, praying he would hear what I had to say. "Even on the cross when He was dying for all of humanity's sin, He was forgiving the people who were nailing Him to the cross. There, under the weight of every sin, He who committed no sin – suffered as though He did… so that you and I don't have to have eternal death.

"He made a way for us to have a new life in Him. We can repent from our sins, be baptized in His Name and receive the Holy Ghost! Having God's Spirit makes all the difference. I don't need drugs or alcoholic to make everything feel okay – God's Spirit is more than enough.

"I want you to experience this, Avery."

He looked wistful, almost hopeful. "That'd be nice."

"Avery, I promised you; now, you promise me." Emotion betrayed my voice and I swiped at a tear that was forming in my eye. "No matter what the judge says – you'll look into this whole God thing. Because Jesus wants to say, 'not guilty'."

I stood. Midway to the door, Avery called after me. I turned around to see the tug of a smile play on the edge of his lips.

"Thanks, Chloe."

***

That night I lay restlessly on my bed. Avery's face kept playing on the screen of my mind. I remembered Gracie's laugh, and the way she cried when Avery didn't come home. I determined to go visit her tomorrow.

I finally got sick of tossing and turning in my bed. I got up and stretched. I threw a sweatshirt on and walked to the window. The stars were so bright, and the moon hung low enough to touch. I wished dad hadn't told me not to sneak out anymore. I'd go to Gracie's house if he hadn't forbidden it. Without giving it much thought, I opened my window, climbed out and sat on the little ledge.

"God, I still have some unanswered questions." I said.

No answer came in the silence of the night. I felt peaceful, even in the middle of my stormy questions.

***

The next morning Dad and Mr. Riley were at the kitchen table. They greeted me, offered me a doughnut, and then asked me to sit down.

"You have been working with ANTI, Action National Teen Interference, to help stop the drug problem in our area. Thanks to you, and a few other agents, we were able to catch Andrew Gillis, the biggest dealer to our teens.

76

Turns out, he was the one transporting the drugs from Chicago."

"Wow. What happened with Avery?"

"Avery has been sent to a halfway house where he will be getting the help he deserves. His sentence was a lot lighter because he helped us with Gillis." Mr. Riley said.

"Did we ever find out who snitched on me?"

"Andrew Gillis put it together. You're trying to join the gang and your dad is a lawyer; it just didn't seem right." Mr. Riley said.

"Oh, won't that cause problems in the future?"

"No, you'll probably never do another mission in your home town. It's too risky. You'll do what Ethan did."

"Ethan?"

"Yes, He's not really a problem kid who got kicked out of school." Mr. Riley leaned back, crossed his arms, and slouched in his seat. "He's the same as you - just a kid of a law agent. This is extremely confidential Chloe. Tomorrow, Ethan is going to be expelled from school and you're not likely to ever see him again. You can never tell a soul."

"Dad, when Ryan and I were kidnapped, I did tell him I was a spy. Though, I told him I was probably fired."

Dad looked concerned. "Just down play it if he ever mentions it. Allow him to think you were fired."

"But on a brighter note," Mr. Riley spoke, "You have successfully completed your first mission. We've recently completed our training for American ANTI training. We're offering you a scholarship."

"Really? That's so awesome!"

"You'll have four semesters at ANTI; then you're off to the college of your choice paid for completely. The only contingent is, you'll be an on-call spy. Are you okay with that?"

"Okay with it?" I asked. "This is the missing puzzle

piece of my life. I feel," I paused thinking for the right word, "Oh, I don't know, identified?"

"That's not a good feeling for a spy to have, Chloe." Dad said.

"I suppose not."

It was quiet in the kitchen for a while. Mr. Riley was going through some paper work in a folder; dad was staring off into the nothingness of the cloudy sky through the window.

Happiness enveloped my heart in a hug; I felt the adventure was only beginning.

Dear Readers,

Thank you so much for joining Chloe's adventure in Identified. I truly hope you have enjoyed reading her story as much as I have enjoyed writing it.

Would you consider writing a short review on Amazon? These reviews help other readers experience Chloe's adventure. As a newer novelist to the market, your review means the world to me and reassures other readers who aren't familiar with my literature.

Thanks, again! & God Bless!

Emily Hemstock

ABOUT THE AUTHOR

Emily Hemstock resides in the Upper Peninsula of Michigan. She has a passion for writing Christian-based books for young readers.

Made in the USA
Columbia, SC
23 May 2019